The Halloween Queen

BY **Joan Holub**

ILLUSTRATED BY **Theresa Smythe**

Albert Whitman & Company, Morton Grove, Illinois

For Katie, Jessica, and Amanda,
whose Halloween parties are a treat!
—J.H.

To my fiendish nieces and nephews:
Maggie and Harry,
Kelly and Sam,
Julia, Jake, and Sean.
—T.S.

Library of Congress Cataloging-in-Publication Data

Holub, Joan.
The Halloween Queen / Joan Holub ; illustrated by Theresa Smythe.
p. cm.
Summary: Even though the Halloween Queen has the best candy on the block and the best decorations,
one young trick-or-treater is scared until a Halloween party changes her mind.
ISBN 0-8075-3138-3 (hardcover)
[1. Halloween—Fiction. 2. Parties—Fiction. 3. Stories in rhyme.] I. Smythe, Theresa, ill. II. Title.
PZ8.3.H74Hal 2004 [E]--dc22 2003026027

It's Halloween night
and Sam shouts from the street:
"Hey, put on your costume!
Let's go trick-or-treat!"

We ring every doorbell. We're not going to stop
'til we've filled our bags to the very tiptop.
But one house is spooky. I try to sneak past.
I don't stop. I don't look. I just run by—fast.

The lady who lives there adores Halloween.
So that's why I call her the Halloween Queen!
Each year in October her flowers turn black.
A ghost haunts her front yard, and bats hang out back.
Wolves howl from her rooftop. Cats hiss from her trees.
A skeleton family sways in the breeze.

The treats she gives out are the best on our block.
Still, I'm scared to go up to her door and knock.
My friends are not frightened. They tap on her door—
knights, mummies, queens, vampires, and witches galore.
The other kids go. One by one. Two by two.
So Sam says I'm chicken. He says, "I dare you!"

I take one step forward. One more after that.
In no time I'm standing on her welcome mat.
My knees are a-knocking. My feet are concrete.
I take a big breath, and I shout:

TRICK-OR-TREAT!

The spookiest person
that I've ever seen
creaks open the door.
It's the Halloween Queen!
Her fangs are quite ghoulish.
She has ruby lips.
Her glittery glasses
have bugs on the tips.

The Halloween Queen croaks, "Hello," with a grin.
Her door opens wider. She says, "Do come in."
Before I can run off, before I can hide,
she reaches out,

grabs me,

and scoops me inside!

I peek through my fingers.
I peer through the gloom.
Weird music and giggles
float all through the room.
I shake and I shiver. Where is everyone?
Then I see my friends . . .

GASP!

They're all having fun!

A Halloween party! Oh, I should have guessed
the Halloween Queen's would of course be the best.

We play pin the sticker on Witch Wanda's nose.
I miss by a mile. I stick mine on her toes.

Sam wraps me in paper—the toilet roll kind.
We turn into mummies, and then we unwind!

We paint pumpkin faces. Some smile and some frown.
Mine looks like a spaceman. Sam's looks like a clown.

There's plenty to snack on. It's time to dig in.
I cannot decide quite where I should begin.
The crabapple goblins all dripping with goo?
Green marshmallow monsters? Some sweet bubbling brew?

The critter-top cupcakes? A popcorn eyeball?
It's too hard to choose one, so I try them all!

The snacks have been snacked on. The games have been played. At last, it is time for a costume parade!

Soon the clock in the hall bongs thirteen sad bongs.
The Halloween Queen croaks out thirteen "so longs!"

As I look behind me, she slips out of sight.
She won't be the same again after tonight.

I'll see her tomorrow. And more after that.
But she won't be wearing her extra-tall hat.
Her teeth won't be green, and her lips won't be red.
Her cackling laughter won't fill me with dread.

The skeleton family won't sway on her lawn.
The ghosts, bats, and goblins will all be long gone.
The Halloween Queen will change from a creature . . .

back into Ms. Green, my favorite teacher!